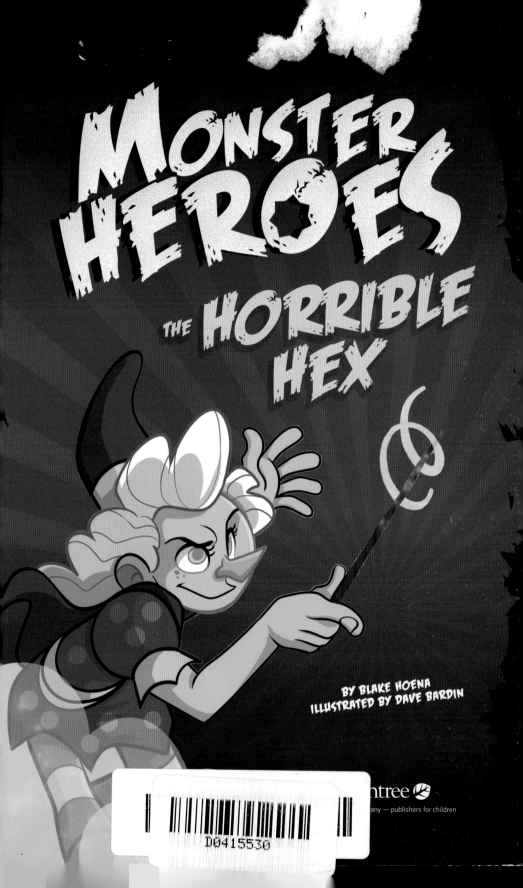

MONSTER HEROES

THE HORRIBLE HEX

BY BLAKE HOENA
ILLUSTRATED BY DAVE BARDIN

ntree
any — publishers for children

Raintree is an imprint of Capstone Global Library Limited, a company incorporated in England and Wales having
its registered office at 264 Banbury Road, Oxford, OX2 7DY – Registered company number: 6695582

www.raintree.co.uk
myorders@raintree.co.uk

Text © Capstone Global Library Limited 2019
The moral rights of the proprietor have been asserted.

Edited by Christianne Jones
Designed by Ted Williams
Original illustrations © Capstone Global Library Limited 2019
Illustrated by Dave Bardin
Production by Kris Wilfahrt
Originated by Capstone Global Library Ltd
Printed and bound in India

ISBN 978 1 4747 6128 4
22 21 20 19 18
10 9 8 7 6 5 4 3 2 1

British Library Cataloguing in Publication Data
A full catalogue record for this book is available from
the British Library.

Acknowledgements
We would like to thank the following for permission to reproduce photographs: Shutterstock: Kasha_malasha,
design elemen: popular business, design element

CONTENTS

MINA (the Vampire)

Mina thinks people taste like dirty socks, so beetroot juice is her snack of choice. Its red colour has fooled her parents into thinking that she's a traditional blood-sucking vampire instead of a superhero. She has the ability to change into a bat or a mouse at will.

Brian is the brainy one amongst his friends. Unlike other zombies, Brian prefers tofu to brains. No matter what sort of trouble is brewing, Brian always comes up with a plan to save the day, like a true superhero.

BRIAN (the Zombie)

WILL *(the Ghost)*

Will is quite shy. Luckily he can become invisible whenever he wants to, because he is a ghost. When Will is doing good deeds, he likes to remain unseen. His invisibility helps him to be brave like a real superhero.

With a wave of her wand and a poetic chant, Linda can reverse any magical curse. She hopes to use her magic to help people, just like a superhero would.

LINDA *(the Witch)*

CHAPTER 1

HEX POTION

KA-BOOM!

Linda jumped out of her seat.

"What was that?" she cried.

Peep. Peep! Petey squeaked.

Petey was Linda's pet. He helped her to do witchy stuff. Only Linda understood what Petey peeped.

"I think you're right, Petey," Linda said. "My sisters, Agnes and Griselda, must be up to no good."

Peep. Peep! Petey squeaked again.

"Okay, let's find out what they're doing," Linda said.

Linda and Petey crept down the stairs one creaky step at a time. They peeked into the kitchen and gasped.

Linda's sisters were huddled around a black cauldron. So were their pets, Slither and Scratch. Smoke filled the room.

Agnes coughed. "Did it work?" she asked.

Griselda coughed too. "I don't know," she said.

Smoke poured out of the cauldron. Then it moved across the floor and under the door.

Slither hissed at the smoke.

Hiss! Hiss!

Scratch growled. *GRRR! GRRR!*

"It worked! The smoke has a life of its own," Griselda screeched.

"Yes, let's see what it does," Agnes cackled.

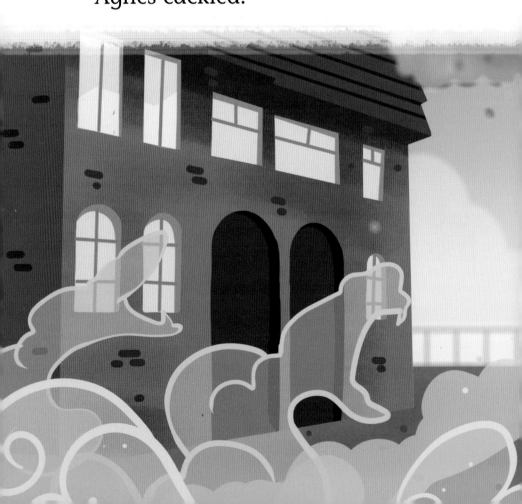

Linda's sisters ran to a window.
Linda did too.

The smoke wormed its way
along the pavement. It sneaked
up behind a boy and grabbed his
foot. The boy tripped, falling into
a bush.

Then the smoke sneaked up to a girl who was licking an ice cream. It knocked the cone to the ground.

"It works! It works!" Agnes laughed.

"Our hex smoke will cause all sorts of problems!" Griselda laughed.

Peep! Peep! Petey squeaked.

"I know," Linda said. "We'd better get some help."

SECRET HIDEOUT

Linda waited for her friends at their hideout in the graveyard.

First Will floated through a window.

"Where's Brian?" he asked.

Then Mina flew in as a bat.

"Zombies are so slow," Mina said.

About an hour later, the trapdoor popped open. Brian crawled in.

Zombies were always late.

"So what's the problem?" Will asked.

Linda told her friends what her sisters were doing.

"Your sisters created a cloud of smoke?" Mina asked.

"And it goes around hurting people?" Brian asked.

Linda nodded. "I know it's weird. But we need to stop it," she said.

Linda and her friends were not like other monsters. They did not want to scare people or hex them. They wanted to be like superheroes and help people.

"But how?" Mina asked.

"Easy," Brian said. "But first we need to find that hex cloud."

Linda and her friends left their hideout. They ran into town. What they saw there was frightening.

In the park, picnickers huddled under wet blankets. The hex cloud poured rain on them.

At the basketball court, players could not get the ball in the net. The hex cloud kept knocking away the ball.

On the playground, the cloud pushed kids up the slide. It spun the roundabout too fast, and kids flew off. It lifted the swings out of reach.

"This is madness!" Will said.

Then Linda saw her sisters.
They were sitting on a bench and
watching what was happening.
They were laughing.

"Okay, it's time for our plan,"
Brian said.

WINGS AND WIND

POOF!

Mina changed into a bat.

Linda pulled out her wand.

She waved at Mina and chanted,

"Hocus-pocus turn humongous!"

Suddenly, Mina began to grow.

She grew from a little black bat

into a huge black bat.

"Now flap your wings," Brian said.

As Mina flapped, she created a gust of wind. The wind blew the smoke away from the picnickers. It pushed the smoke off the basketball court. It drove the smoke from the playground.

"Now blow the smoke at Agnes and Griselda," Brian said.

Mina blew the smoke towards Linda's sisters. Will helped direct the smoke by waving his sheet. Linda helped by waving her wand.

First the smoke made the bench they were sitting on collapse. *THUD!* Agnes and Griselda fell to the ground.

Then it pulled their pointy hats over their heads.

"Hey, I can't see!" Griselda shouted.

"We need to get out of here!" Agnes cried.

Slither hissed and Scratch growled in agreement.

The sisters started to run off. Mina continued to blow the smoke after them.

It grabbed their feet, and they fell into a bush.

It lifted Scratch and Slither into the air. The witches grabbed their pets to stop them from flying away.

The sisters ran into their house and huddled around the cauldron. They made another spell to reverse the smoke.

Thankfully it worked straight away. Linda and her friends laughed.

"That will teach them to make such mean hexes," Linda said.

"It certainly will!" Mina said.

Agnes and Griselda just moaned from the kitchen.

DAVE BARDIN

Dave Bardin studied illustration while working as an art teacher. As an artist, Dave has worked on many different projects for television, books, comics and animation. In his spare time Dave enjoys watching documentaries, listening to podcasts, travelling and spending time with friends and family.

BLAKE HOENA

Blake Hoena grew up in Wisconsin, USA, where he wrote stories about robots conquering the Moon and trolls lumbering around the woods behind his house. He now lives in Minnesota, USA, and continues to write about fun things such as space aliens and superheroes. Blake has written more than fifty chapter books and graphic novels for children.

GLOSSARY

cauldron large pot, often associated with witches' brews

chant say or sing a phrase again and again

graveyard place where dead people are buried

hex magical spell that is meant to cause bad luck for someone

hideout place where someone hides to avoid being found or captured

reverse turn back

TALK ABOUT IT

1. Linda and her friends don't want to cause trouble. They want "to be like superheroes and help people". If you could be a superhero, what would your superpower be? Would you use it to help people?

2. The Monster Heroes have a secret hideout in the graveyard. If you could have a secret hideout, where would it be? What would it look like?

3. If you were Linda, what would you say to your sisters? Would you try to explain why what they did was wrong?

WRITE ABOUT IT

1. Use your imagination and write the recipe for a potion. Make sure you write out how much of each ingredient the potion needs and name it.

2. The group solves their problem by turning Mina into a giant bat whose wings can control the smoke. What are other ways they could have stopped the sisters' smoke from getting out of control?

3. Would you rather be a witch, a vampire, a zombie or a ghost? Write a paragraph explaining your answer.